# There's an Angel On Your shoulder

Eric C. Stirrup

ISBN: 978-1-9164903-4-5

GeekyGirl Publishing

I have to thank my two children, Jonathan and Rebecca, for getting me writing and the continual encouragement from my wife Jacqui. It was Christmas 2000 when something my son said, got me going. Ever since I have been taken captive by pen and paper and a vivid imagination that has caused me to draw upon past experiences and feel the loss that others have felt. I have stood in their shoes, felt their pain and laughed with them.

But most of all, it is the inspiration I have found through Yahweh.

Thanks to David Davies and Ruth Alliston for your reviews and feedback:

'A word aptly spoken is like
apples of gold in setting silver'
Proverbs 25 v 11

Eric's poetry and stories make me smile, think or cry. If I had a flower for every time he made me laugh, I would have a garden to walk in forever - Jacqui.

* * *

I remember my dad telling me that he couldn't write poetry because of the whole rhyming thing. I told him that poetry didn't have to rhyme, and he decided to give it a go. Twenty-years later and he is a prolific writer of both poems and stories, and I can't help but notice that all of his poems tend to rhyme!

My dad puts himself into everything he writes. His stories and his poetry are always heartfelt and beautiful. And I am sure you will love his book - Rebecca.

* * *

My dad has always been an inspiration. A word smith non pareil. When he discovered poetry he discovered a door and a play space on the other side that we now get to enjoy from the park bench at the side. From the shade we watch our dad gambol and amble from one drift of expression to the next; and, I love it - Jonathan.

Contents

*The Great Commission*

The young, and somewhat undisciplined, junior angel was called to cloud 716 to face another severe dressing down from his Mentor. He just could not maintain the levels of concentration worthy of an angel. He had only narrowly passed Angel Training School. Tillic was always interrupting and asking too many questions. Several times he turned up late for class. His excuses varied but mostly centred on being on some great quest, doing a great deed rescuing one of the Elite.

He wondered why he had been chosen. What, if any, gift he had? He didn't much like the name he was given: 'Tillic'. It didn't exactly roll off the tongue, it was hardly cool. It was the Mentor who had made the final decision and Tillic wondered why. When the Mentor took a training class Tillic was prone to fall asleep. Now when Gideon took a lesson, Tillic was the first one there. Gideon was the leader of The Elite. He talked about tactics, and battles and victories against The Fallen. He talked of brave deeds and sacrifice and Tillic always found himself on the edge of his seat.

When it came to weapon practice, he was top of his class. He so wanted wings like Gideon's: bright feathers, colours that dimmed all others. When Tillic was first fitted with *his* wings, he had thought they would come full of feathers. But no. The feathers had to grow as he progressed through Angel school and Junior Angel Status. The depth of colours only came with an intensity of understanding.

Before meeting The Mentor, Tillic thought it best to review his record.

- kindness - *fair*;
- patience - *very poor*;
- love - *very poor*;

- gentleness - *fair*;
- peace – *poor*:
- joy - *excellent*;
- faithfulness - *very good*;
- self-control - *very poor*;
- goodness - *good*.

He was in trouble. You needed high marks in all areas to advance as an Angel, and he so wanted to be a Warrior Angel and go on missions with Gideon. Tillic just didn't get all this touchy-feely stuff. What was the point?

He entered the Great Hall and took a sharp left. Tillic approached The Mentor's abode and his pace slowed. He did love The Mentor. Tillic knew there was something very special about him. The rumours held that, without the Mentor, the rebellion may have succeeded. He stood a full nine-feet tall and, as imposing as that was, it was nothing compared to the way he looked at you and into you. He seemed able to see things that you could not see yourself and you were left trembling inside.

Tillic hoped that his wings wouldn't be removed, as shabby as they were. He had spent some time that morning preening them to look their best. The door to the chamber opened as Tillic approached.

On exiting he was full of relief despite poor assessment. He had been given a field Commission. Tillic could hardly believe it with his record! The Commission may have been 'the least attractive of all commissions', but it was his last chance to succeed as a Fully Fledged angel. Tillic was to be sent to a distant planet known as earth, to: 'look, observe, and report back on what moved him and touched his emotions most'.

He had to hitch a lift across two galaxies before arriving at the least of all planets, and he could already feel his wings (or what there was of them) droop. Angel school only devoted one day to planet earth, such was its insignificance and history of violence. Tillic, therefore, arrived with no expectations and took a quick tour round the various continents, sending back regular reports, only to be told to 'try harder'. Eventually Tillic hid himself in a small coastal English town. He was sitting on a park bench overlooking a pond. He liked this spot, he often sneaked up and stole swan feathers in an attempt to repair his own.

Boredom drove him to try and concentrate and he soon found himself watching a man called Brian. Tillic did not know why he started to watch the man. Perhaps it was the slouch as Brian walked, his bowed head, the picture of dejection and failure. Yes, Tillic recognised that feeling.

So Tillic sat on Brian's left shoulder and began listening to Brian's thoughts and feelings. A darkness descended over him as he started to assimilate some of Brian's inner feelings. A sense of loss and hopelessness. It wasn't just his feelings. He smelt. Didn't know that did you. Yes, Angels can smell. He soon pulled out a feather from his wing and shaped it into a quill and began to write on his left hand. In doing this it immediately transferred to his mentor. I know what you are thinking, 'how does this work'? Well, there are some things I can tell you and some things I can't. This is one of the latter, so live with it.

*Priscilla The Pigeon*

Brian had left the funeral in a sober and reflective mood. In his pocket lay a crumpled letter left him by his wife, Lisa. It had been like a knife in his heart. He had been made to look in the mirror and see how his passion had robbed him of what should have been his true passion. The letter had set in motion things that had lain dormant in him for years, and now started to break through the surface and fracture his hard exterior. At home he opened the letter again. The junior angel peered over his shoulder and read with him.

*Brian my love,*

Hold my hands, hold them tight, I want to feel your calluses, scratches, cuts and bumps. They were hard earned those knots and lumps; they came at a price. Tools found their home in those hands of yours. They moulded themselves together with you, they became an extension of you, and you they. You belonged together like a man and his lover made for each other. I envied those tools in your hand; you caressed them like a lover caresses his lost love. They shaped and carved things of beauty. Oak, beech, walnut, cedar and rosewood, they were your lovers each one your mistress. The hours you spent with them rather than me. How you looked at them with longing, their fragrance would linger on you. I knew each night who it was you had been with before lying with me. The cabinet you made, the shelves carved with such love, the table and chairs you would look and look at, and for you time stood still. I hated the attention you gave to them and not to me. You never looked at me with such passion, never stroked my hair the way you rubbed your hands over your finished work. I was never rubbed with oil and admired like them.

Oh, but I do love your hands, big and strong and so gentle when you caress my breast, so strong when you pick me up and draw me near to you. Your hands comfort me, they give me hope, make me feel secure, they lift me up when I fall down. I want to brush the sawdust off your trousers, pick bits of wood chipping out of your hair and smell your lovers. I know time is short, I've said goodbye to all my family and friends but have reserved you to the last. The doctors have made their last visit, left me to choose when the time has come. But I want my last memory to be your callused hands holding me close.

Tillic sent his report and the mentor's reply came more quickly than before: 'Stay listen and learn'.

Tools, the fragrance of wood had lost their beauty to Brian, the urge to create something out of what some believed to be dead and breathe life into it had gone since Lisa had said goodbye. Reluctantly, Brian found himself at a therapist's as he looked for answers to his anguish. The junior angel listened to all that transpired.

'You know what you need? You need to learn to love again,' said the therapist, in his laid-back know-it-all way with his 'been there done that' emblazoned over his t-shirt. Tillic listened to Brian's thoughts and feelings:

All of thirty-three; the been there, done it therapist, five years in his mother's arms, twenty years in education, three years back-packing, two years shelf filling; this supercilious self-made twit sat there and said, 'You need to learn to love again'. The veins in Brian's neck began to bulge with anger, his face reddened. Fists clenched tight; white knuckles on display to the laid back, know-it-all with designer ripped jeans, three-day-stubble, flip flops and strong coffee beside him.

Brian grabbed the table and threw it across the room: cold coffee, nibbles and books scattered around the floor; the chair flew across the room next. Brian roared his pain and the therapist sought protection under his desk. The junior angel fell off Brian's shoulder and had to hold on to his trousers.

Brian needed air; he needed to breathe. Sweat broke out on his brow and invaded every crevice, his mouth as dry as a crushed leaf in winter. Outside, he headed for the park; cars skidded to a halt to avoid this suicidal, couldn't-care-less man, ice-cold inside and locked up in despair. Tillic had to intervene twice to prevent a catastrophic incident. This was something Tillic had been taught in angel school never to do, but then he never listened to his teachers.

The park. The space. Too much space. Too many staring people. Couples holding hands, a child carried on her father's shoulders; laughter and play all around, a dog trotting along with a prized stick in its mouth and its tail held high. All too much for the distraught man.

The wood beckoned and, after that, the bridge. Leaves crushed beneath his feet like eggshells, the bare and barren branches mirrored his soul and the snow, in flakes the size of ten-pence pieces, began to fall.

Brian stood on the bridge, looking into the flowing water making its way to the open sea, beckoning it. Such peace and calm invited Brian to join them. Just then a squirrel ran across his path chased by a Yorkshire Terrier, pursued by a distraught woman.

She shouted, 'Womble! Stay Womble.'

Brian looked at the scene and the lure of the river dissipated. The snow and the wind blew Brian home. The curtains remained drawn; each room was shrouded in a layer of dust. A pile of unwashed dishes littered the living room; the table, draining board and sink already full. The bin spewed out its contents. The night came. The snow fell as Brian drifted nearer to hell and the darkness inside. Hunger drove him to the fridge with too little in it. Friends had stopped visiting and bringing food. The phone was full of unanswered messages. The pantry revealed nothing but a small bag of muesli and long-life milk. It would have to do. The junior angel felt Brian's hunger.

Necessity drove Brian to the sink to wash the dishes. Looking out of the window, the snow lay thick, icy wind whistled through every crevice. A pigeon landed on the fence opposite the kitchen window and shivered with a look of desperation. Not knowing why, Brian opened the window. The pigeon flew inside and fell into the warm, soapy water. Brian found a towel, picked her up and wrapped it round her. He placed her in front of the fire and quickly lit it. He dried the exhausted bird; it looked at him, hopefully. Brian retrieved an empty box and layered it with strips of unread newspaper and an old jumper, and gently placed her inside. All night he watched over this fragile, cold, lost bird. And as he watched he began to tidy and clean the rubbish, not willing to offend his visitor. Left over pizza and curry containers, cans of beer and unread post began to disappear. Dust ridden shelves and surfaces were cleaned and the curtains opened. Then the pigeon began to stir. A dish of muesli and water were placed before his guest in front of the warm and inviting fire.

After a while, and with some encouragement, she ate and drank before jumping back into her cosy box and sleeping.

Cleaning the house revealed a picture placed face down for two-weeks. The love of his life. Brian had been unable to look at it. Over the next three-days, the pigeon grew in strength, and followed Brian from room to room, as if checking up on him.

First she walked, then she took short flights and, once, landed on his right shoulder; the left one was occupied by the junior angel.

The snow stopped and the wind ceased and Priscilla the pigeon (that's what Brian had named her) began to look out of the window and back at him. Time, he thought, to let her go. He opened the window three times, she looked at the sky and back at him as if reluctant to leave him alone.

Finally he said, 'It's okay Priscilla, you belong out there, the sky is your home.' She walked to the open window and, with one glance back, she launched herself into the sky; with her, something of Brian departed. The junior angel envied the pigeon; he longed to fly.

Two days later, wrapped up warm, the fridge and pantry now full, and having looked for a long time at his wife's picture, Brian entered the world. The snow had mostly melted away and the park beckoned; with hot coffee and a pain au chocolate he sat at their bench to watch the world go by. Memories lived there. Brian sat on the bench overlooking the lake. Boats sailed, the winches gently tapping their masts.

Brian looked up and saw a pigeon circle, (the junior angel longed to soar unseen with the pigeon). Eventually it landed on Brian's left shoulder and tugged at his woolly hat. She shared some of his food, and then was gone. Something broke inside Brian and he began to weep. Deep groans came from somewhere within. All the hurt, the anger, the feeling of loss, began to wash away.

A woman with her dog had watched the scene: a shaking man. She came and sat by his side. The uncontrollable sobs could not be stemmed. Warm hands enfolded his, and soft words found open ears.

'It will be okay,' she said, 'it will be okay.' Her dog began to nuzzle Brian's legs.

He choked back tears and his trembling voice said, 'I'm okay. I'm just learning to love again'.

*Pillow Talk*

Tillic jumped from Brian's shoulder to listen in on the lady. Her name was Mary. Tillic began to feel strange, and his dreams of war and righteous battles waned. Something he could not quite understand started to grow inside him. Something about Mary attracted him. It was the way she had held Brian's hands, as if she already knew his story, felt his brokenness, the sickness of his soul.

Had Tillic discerned something of what his Mentor had sent him here for? He felt light-headed and his feathers began to grow. Tillic marvelled at his plumage and plucked another feather to begin a new report.

Mary continued to hold Brian's hands as long as he needed. She had lost someone too. When Brian left, she looked at the inscription on the bench. Her husband had made it a long time ago; Mary stared and Tillic started to explore her loss.

Mary had written her feelings down and, from time to time, the words came to her mind. Brian's loss had triggered her memory, and words tumbled in her head and as they fell Tillic caught each and every one.

Age forty-two, no children. Detached house in a small cul-de-sac. She had been left well-off. Insurance policies, her husband's pension and the sale of her parents' house, had left her financially secure, but not emotionally. There was a chasm inside her heart that she filled with fantasy. Her pretence of being OK was a thin veneer.

Mary, Tillic learned, had found her own way of coping with her loss and had resisted the temptation of visiting a therapist. Instead, she'd talked with friends, shook her fist at an unknown enemy, swearing with rage. Each day she had her own strategy and this morning had been the same.

Tillic had begun feeling an urge to fly but was drawn into Mary's nightly experience and how she coped. The junior angel observed it all as he lay by her side and continued to write; he entered her dreams, her thoughts, her feelings. And as she awoke from her sleep her fantasy became more real. This was a weekly ritual that she savoured.

The morning light broke through the blinds and fell upon his picture; Mary looked to remember what once was. She rolled over and saw his place next to her. Always on her right near to the light and closest to the door, so as not to disturb her when he woke early for work. And there it was, the shape of a head pressed into the pillow. She created that last night. Mary imagined him there with his tussled hair, her arm sneaking between his arm and bare chest, playing with the hairs on his chest as he awakes with a start, looks at the clock and leaps out of bed fumbling for his dressing gown.

The memory lingers. Then he has gone. She misses those moments. The farting too, although he said he never heard hers. The smelly ones she could do without and yet she would welcome them back just to know he was there. His shaving set was still in the bathroom with his favourite aftershave. She would open it at least once a week just to imagine he was still there. She had given lots of his stuff away but kept his favourite suit and shirt and that tie he liked so much, a present for his fortieth. There were lots of things she still did just for him. The 'belly buster breakfast' once a month at 10 o clock, on a Saturday morning. She always settled for muesli or porridge, although she loved to see him tuck in: crispy bacon, one sausage prepared by their butcher, mushrooms picked fresh from their secret place, two fried runny eggs and a slice of toast. It would be there this morning. She had it all ready. She did it for the smell, it filled the kitchen and the other rooms, and then she would see him.

Ready for work, he never failed to hold her head gently in his hands, kissing both her closed eye lids, rubbing her nose with his, the back of his left hand would fall onto her right breast and she would feel his wedding ring through her silk pyjama top. She used to savour that moment until she heard the front door shut and the car pull off the drive.

Tonight, she was going to make his favourite meal. There would be a place laid for him opposite her. A bottle of their best wine poured into two glasses. She would imagine him there. Sometimes, when she began to lose his features, she waited till very late, wrapped up warm and walked to the cemetery and stood at his grave talking. It made her feel better, and then the slow walk back. She had encountered a tramp in the graveyard. Tucked up by the low wall, sheltered from the wind. She found it comforting to know her husband was not alone.

Friends kept coming round, worrying when they found her happy and content. They advised a grief counsellor, sent her tickets for a play, invited her on their holiday not wanting her to be alone. And she would think, *when did you last have your eyelids kissed, your nose rubbed, your lips caressed?*

Every day she felt him near, his touch when he wiped away her tears. *They don't make belly buster breakfasts for their men. Share a glass of wine across a table just for two. So,* she thought, *you can stick your therapy gurus who wanted her to wake up and come back to the real world. No thanks, she would stay in her own world where she could still feel loved.*

Tillic felt that she needed to find freedom but, at the same time, he envied her isolation and memories. As he began to empathise, yes empathise, with Mary and her loss, his wings began to grow, and he began to preen his feathers and spread his wings. He would spread them wide and compare them with the swans he had so admired. The strange thing about his feathers, was that they began to take on different colours. The reds got stronger, the greens deeper and then, the most coveted of all, the purple deepened. It gave him an extraordinary feeling of elation.

Oh, I know what some of you think. You think all angel feathers are white. Well, some are but the coloured ones were the most powerful. It was the deep coloured feathers that the fallen angels feared most.

Tillic began to work extra hard leaping from Brian and Mary to experience more of their feelings and make them his own. He felt drunk with earthly emotions. He lay down on soft leaves, smelt the moss could taste the air, soft and fresh. He felt a small creature crawl over his hand, his feathers began to sing, and he felt warm, oh so warm. A mole broke the surface of the ground as if to see what all the fuss was about, and then returned to its burrow.

Slowly he returned to himself and was anxious to continue his quest. He caught up with both Mary and Brian and wondered if it was by accident or if there was some special reason.

*Born to be happy*

Mary and Brian found themselves going to the same funeral.

Mary had been a babysitter, on occasions, for a young girl. Brian had been her uncle. Both felt obliged to come but had no real desire to do so. They had suffered their own loss.

They both new the story of Vicky and Clare.

Tillic found himself busily jumping from one shoulder to the other to unravel the story, it required a succession of feathers and quills and his hand began to ache with so much writing. He pieced the story together to make his report.

Tillic began to feel drained and faint. He wished he had never entered into human emotions, as their pain began to overwhelm him. Brian and Mary had no idea that they would meet at such an event. When Mary spied Brian her first urge was to leave. But she was curious, why was he here? Then the service began, and she thought of Vicky.

Vicky had a baby girl. She'd met a lad at Uni, and then was left on her own with a new gift. Not an unusual story. But this mom and daughter, Vicky and Clare, would prove to be different. At age three, Clare was diagnosed with cancer, a curse for the aged but for a child facing years of treatment, emotional highs and lows, hope deferred making the heart grow weary, being dragged from specialist to specialist, some new drug, a better treatment, trawling the net for a cure, faithful friends waiting for news, words of encouragement, a hug, a kiss, a hidden tear, a broken heart. a bald head hidden by a coloured scarf, family and friends lending support, sympathised, empathised, this could break anyone. Not Clare. She and her mom refused to be the centre of others' anxiety.

In this Vicky found an ally, his name was Robo, an old friend from uni. Whenever he visited (which was frequent) Clare would get excited. He would come in, pick her up, whizz her around, throw her in the air, wrestle with her, carry her on his shoulders and charge around in a demented way until, exhausted, both would collapse and laugh and laugh and laugh. They would, all three, go out and discover something new in everything they saw. Every day became an adventure for Clare and her mom, and they agreed together to do at least one new fun thing a day. Pillow fights, bouncing up and down on the bed, seeing a cartoon, playing on the beach, have her friends' round. They threw themselves into every new day. No one but no one was allowed to be sad with Clare around. All this in-between treatments, tests, physical weakness, the cancer gaining ground.

Clare, age nine, died 23rd March 2018 in America, while having treatment for an aggressive cancer.

One day, on hearing her grandmother and mother talking about why and what they were here for, she had interrupted them to say, 'I know why I am here'.

'Why are you here Clare?' her mother asked.

'I'm here because God wants me to make people happy,' she'd replied.

For years people had prayed for Clare to be healed, and instead found love, love in abundance, in her smile, her joy, her fun and yes, in seeing her make people happy. Her funeral was filled with colour, no one was allowed to wear sombre clothes, everything worn had to reflect the impact this child had on them. They all wore coloured clothes. Brian sat in the church next to a little girl. Mary was two rows behind. Brian turned to the little girl, who was weeping.

'Did you know Clare?' he asked.

'She was my best friend', she said, 'she always made me laugh.' They wept together as they saw a small white coffin being transported down the aisle, carried by four young men unashamedly shaking and crying as they held their precious cargo. A pigeon had found its way into the church, flew round and landed on the coffin. A steward went to remove it but a restraining hand held him back. The funeral was full of friends and family weeping and loving each other.

Clare's mother stood at the front of the church, looking out at this vast array of people with standing room only and said, 'When Clare was dying, she prayed to God and He came into the room and filled it with love.' Vicky could not find words to explain just how big was this, the love of God.

Afterwards Mary and Brian had assembled with others in a large room for tea, coffee and cake. Robo was there with Vicky's mother deep in conversation they hugged and sobbed. Tillic thought to go and listen in but decided to leave it. He sensed that this Robo had his own story to tell and thought he would return to sit on his shoulder but for now he was taken up in the moment and an atmosphere that he was getting too close to. There were tears, laughter and lots and lots of hugs. They had all shared this journey with Vicky and Clare. The one thing that dominated the whole assembly were memories of the times Clare made them laugh and, even with tear-stained swollen cheeks, mascara washed away, there was laughter and joy outweighing the hurt. It was the most unforgettable, unbelievable experience of a little girl who gave to people more than they asked for and more than they believed they deserved. She had made them happy.

Tillic began to feel something he had never felt before. Feathers fell from his wings and mingled with the many tears that ran down cheeks. More feathers grew in their place with brighter colours. Some mingled together giving a rainbow effect. They were fuller than any he had seen before and brighter, and Tillic wondered why. He quickly joined Brian and Mary as they left the church, seeking some solace for himself.

Brian and Mary left together and talked of the love they had known and the love they had lost. A light awakened inside them, as they realised how much they had only valued what they had, now that it was gone. They couldn't get the love of a mother and daughter out of their minds, and just how much Vicky and Clare had had in such a short time together.

Brian and Mary realised that they, too, had received more than they had asked for and more than they had deserved. They walked past their parked cars and continued down to the sea, staying there for most of the afternoon. A sea breeze wafted over them. As they held each other's hand, a bond began to be formed and they felt alive.

Tillic sat in an ancient oak tree and communed with it, savouring its history. The oak had once shared this space with ash, willow and rosewood. It missed them. Tillic pondered all this and sent his report.

His Mentor replied full of praise. Tillic was free to come back or stay to see how the story evolved. Tillic chose to stay.

He began to love spreading his wings, now full of plumage and multi-coloured, allow Earth's wind to lift him into the sky. He wanted to fly with Priscilla and her friends and see what else he could feel, explore and sense on this obscure planet earth. Something had changed in him as he felt a glow inside that wanted to reach out and touch those in need.

*Jigsaw*

Tillic left Brian and Mary to their new adventure. He pottered about near to the lake where he'd first met Mary and enjoyed spreading his wings and preening them. The frost had gone and with it the chill north wind. Crocuses had come and gone, and tulips danced across the ground, as a gentle breeze seemed to play to hidden music.

Tillic followed Robo but then spied a milkman on his round and saw a line of milk-bottles left unused at the door of a house that seemed filled with remorse. He entered the house and found himself sitting in the home of a recently bereaved man. Sixty-six and lonely.

* * *

There he was a picture of rejection looking for someone to blame. It's been three weeks and I still feel the same. That is, I don't feel. Just a numbness inside that I try to hide. I've shook their hands, received their hugs and kisses. Heart-felt, but they left me cold because you were no longer there. It's now five weeks on. Our friends visit less, the phone calls too; they can no longer speak to you.

Yesterday an old friend dropped by with a jigsaw puzzle. He didn't stay long. Told me it would help me find myself, put myself back together. I've crossed him off my Christmas Card list. It's now seven weeks on and this sad old man is staring at the jigsaw, I've tipped all the pieces out; it's three-feet wide and round. I've cleared the rounded table, and spent an afternoon trying to locate what goes where.

It's now day four of doing the jigsaw and I have just managed to complete the outer circle. I punched the air. It's only taken me about thirty-hours. It's now week three of doing the jigsaw, and I have four sections, like floating islands attached to nothing and I've been stuck for two days. I feel like giving up.

Fred popped in for a cup of tea and a chat. How are you, are you managing, do you need any help, blah, blah, blah, blah. Couldn't wait for him to go. He put his coat on and glanced at my failed jigsaw.

'You've got some in the wrong place. Look, that shouldn't be connected to that, you've forced it to fit. If you took that section out, you'll be able to put those together'.

With that he left, and I stared at my mistake. Half an hour later, I had made a great leap forward and completed a large amount. I could see the end in sight.

I was just putting the key in the door, after my weekly shop when Joan and her husband pulled up in their car. I wasn't going to invite them in; I found her a bit bossy. She launched into me, telling me to pull myself together, to stop grieving and that is not what you would have wanted me to be like. I responded in kind with two fingers in the air.

With steam coming out of me ears I charged into the house and slammed the shopping bags down on the table, scattering a large proportion of the jigsaw around. The room was suddenly full of expletives and remorse. I collected all of the broken parts and spent the next six-hours restructuring my circular Jigsaw. Exhausted, I fell asleep in the chair.

It was now just over four-weeks since I started, and the finishing line was approaching. The whole thing was a picture of four seasons, one blending into another. It was a thing of absolute beauty. Except on what should have been the last day of putting the jigsaw together, there was one missing piece. I trawled the floor, spending a long time on my hands and knees, feeling in every crevice.

I could not believe that having worked so hard at putting together this amazing jigsaw that one piece would be absent. Anyone looking at it wouldn't see the pattern, the beauty, how one scene blended into the other. It would be, 'where is the missing piece?' The jigsaw had been my salvation. I felt I had been putting my life back together with each section and all I could see now was the missing piece.

I have now been thirteen weeks on my own, the jigsaw remains unfinished and I've started going out and socialising. I have even begun to smile. But there was still this nagging feeling of not being whole. Another shopping trip. I donate something to someone selling the Big Issue. Then I buy a sandwich and drink for a beggar, I fuss a dog and pass a few pleasantries with people I know. I've even started to have kind thoughts towards Joan and thought I should ring and apologise.

I get home and start emptying the bags of shopping and there it is, the missing piece, in the bottom of the bag. I grab it like some lost treasure and rush to complete the jigsaw. I stand in awe of this wonderful creation, and it's some minutes before I feel wet tears falling off the edge of my chin. Suddenly I feel whole. The journey of putting together 'Autumn' made me explore how I felt when you came back from the specialists, and then your hair began to fall like the leaves from the trees. Then I started on 'Winter' and felt the coldness in my soul as you drifted away, leaving me alone. I hesitated before starting on 'Spring'; I could not imagine a springtime without you ever again. But slowly seeds that others had sown in my life began to germinate and I felt its warmth. I found myself in 'Summertime' and the picture was complete and whole. The last piece of the jigsaw I placed in was the sun in the summertime, and I now felt that whatever season I found myself in without you, would all now have meaning and give me hope.

Before the Junior Angel returned to his mentor, he did one last thing. He wanted to know how Brian and Mary got on.

*Agapae*

Tillic asked his Mentor to allow him to see Brian and Mary in the future, and how their lives wove together. The Mentor permitted the request, he knew that Tillic needed to see one more thing to write his own story. So Tillic was allowed to fast-forward time and view the first two friends that had set him on his journey of discovery.

Tillic plucks a final feather from his plumes to make his last report:

While I sat in Café Revive observing the flow of the human race, I was
Blessed to see a work of grace. Deep, deep love there on display for those who
Would observe. I was drawn to this love called agapae exposed and on
Display, it's something that from time to time we are privileged to see.
It speaks to the inner man and it spoke to me.

The woman who was in no rush as her man in his wheelchair she had to push. She found a table, made a space by removing the unwanted chair and there she positioned her man and brushed back his hair. She bent and whispered in his ear and sniffed, drawing a smile that embraced his wife and made me ponder and wonder, what words drew that love from her man. You could tell from the touch, the smile that these two had walked life's road for many, many miles. His eyes never left her as she ordered coffee and cake, a napkin she secures in his open necked shirt, he begins to sway and in slow time his head droops falling forward, unable to stop. Gentle hands reach out and lovingly push him back into his seat, his dignity restored. Her smile, a gentle touch, soft embracing words bring forth a chuckle and a very broad grin.

She places some cake in his hands; he struggles to lift this morsel to satisfy his taste buds. But agapae love found a way, she encourages, he responds, and the cake finds its home, this is love exposed. Eros and phileo come a poor second, for this is so much deeper for sower and reaper.

The scene repeated time and again, the falling head, a gentle touch, soft words, an amusing smile, a cheeky glance, and then their eyes begin to dance.

Those nearby give an embarrassed look, envying their love dance. Each touch excites the watcher, the hair pushed back out of his eyes, she looks at her man, no words are spoken for all that could be said has been said in the touch, the smile, a chuckle, a word whispered in a willing ear, the twinkling eyes saying, 'I love you dear.' The dance goes on, agapae on display, exposed and envied by all who dared to look, and for me it made me pray, 'God grant me this deep, deep love called agapae.'

Tillic new that this was not the end of the story and he vowed to return. In the meantime, he decided to, do a few loops, climb high in the sky and dive at speed. On a downward flight he viewed an old man and hovered.

As he hovered gently above the old man, his wings disturbed the last leaf on an old oak tree, and it began to shiver. He decided to land on the fence and listen the old man's thoughts, and he was glad that he did.

*The Ancient Oak*

The old man leaned on decaying wooden fencing; he watched the last leaf fall from the great oak. He had climbed this ancient oak as a lad. He picked up the fallen leaf, curled and brown. It had resisted the worst of the storms, refusing to let go. And yet, now, a gust of wind as gentle as a kiss carried it to the ground, amidst a cluster of crocuses. He struggled to bend down and pick it up. The leaf unfolded in his hand; his finger followed the contours, like veins travelling the surface of the leaf. He thought of his reflection in the bathroom mirror that morning. He'd traced the lines in his face, trying to remember what he once looked like. His muscled body, now given over to gravity, only made presentable when covered by carefully styled clothes. He had survived a world war, three battles, shrapnel in his left shoulder, two missing fingers on his right hand, the loss of his wife and his youngest son.

The heart attack had taken its toll, and recovery had been slow, extending his life only to see his family and friends move far away, leaving him alone. He lifted his head and invited the gentle kiss of death to come and take him home.

The wind did not come, and he bowed his head and wept. He struggled on, to his empty flat, his stick supporting each step. As he turned onto the well-worn, weather beaten track he was struck down by a Great Dane in full flow. It sent him spinning out of control, his stick flew into the air, and he fell into a muddy pool. He lay there as the surprised dog came and sniffed the old man's face and arms. It suddenly looked up as it heard its mistress' call. A young woman came running, secured the dog and bent down to check the old man. She stroked the old man's face and whispered into his ear, not realising his hearing aid lay in the mud.

The old man's head slowly raised and turned, like a reluctant reader hesitating to turn the page. He tried to focus but his head was a fog.

As he clenched his fist he felt the leaf in his hand, and he started to recover his thoughts; his sudden longing to be kissed by the wind was replaced by an urge to survive and to get up, embarrassed for having fallen. Slowly, and with some help, he was able to sit awkwardly, supported by the loveliest looking young lady, pouring out a stream of apologies that he could hardly hear. He called out for his glasses and hearing aid. She quickly found his mud-stained glasses. One of the arms was broken, and as he balanced the glasses on the bridge of his nose, they teetered awkwardly on his nose. His hearing aid took a little longer to find. It was caked in mud so he couldn't use it. She kept speaking, and he kept trying to understand what she was saying. A series of hand jesters caused some understanding to emerge between the two. With help, he stood and leaned on his stick, supported by the willing arm of the young woman. The Great Dane danced around them, eager to say sorry to the old man and secure his forgiveness.

He was walked home on unsteady feet to his front door; the sun began to set and night was invited to replace the day. He soon realised that his front door keys could not be found. The night made it impossible for the young lady to return to the site of their encounter and the cold was beginning to bite. He willingly let himself be helped to her home and was glad to sit in her chair by a log fire. She brought a bowl of warm water, a flannel and towel and placed a mirror in front of the old man to aid him in cleaning his muddy face. He appreciated this, as he needed to restore his dignity. He looked at his face in the mirror. The mud had filled his crevices and he looked somewhat better than he had that morning.

His shoulders began to shake and the young lady, who was busy washing his hearing aid, felt waves of compassion for him. She walked silently back to him, prepared to hold him in her arms, only to find that he was chuckling as he looked at his face in the mirror. She held his hand and joined in and soon their laughter became uncontrollable. The Great Dane, who had found his space close to the log fire, lifted his head, as if offended by this sudden change in atmosphere. Through more sign language and mouthed words, they exchanged the strangest of dialogues. A hot cup of tea with a tot of whiskey was a welcome sight and quickly followed by a second. The young lady gave the old man a tour of her home and showed him the spare room, insisting he stay the night. She supplied him with some toiletries and a large nightdress left behind by her mother. More laughter followed. They ate sandwiches and pickles and as his eyes began to droop, she helped him to the spare room and left him to change for bed. Sometime later she tapped the door and entered the spare room with a glass of hot milk. There was no need, the old man was fast asleep. He slept peacefully for the first time in many years and dreamt of the battles he had fought in, his wife and estranged family. He even dreamt of the ancient oak. He'd kissed his first love beneath its branches. They had lain in the sun and planned to meet again, but never did. His disappointment at losing her still haunted him.

He awoke, feeling his shoulder being gently shaken. It took him a while to realise where he was and smiled into the face of the young lady. Stood by her side was a bespectacled middle-aged man. The old man having, relocated his washed and dried hearing aid, soon found that the bespectacled man was her doctor.

The old man could not quite believe that he had slept for a full twelve hours, which was unheard of in his later years. He was given a thorough check. He had multiple bruises, a suspected cracked rib and mild concussion. A discussion between the doctor and the young lady resulted in the old man being persuaded to stay a few days until he felt recovered. Following an afternoon walk with her dog, an excited lady came back waving a bunch of keys in her hand. The old man smiled. The young lady was soon off to his flat, retrieving items of clothing, memorable pictures and some books. The old man still found it difficult to concentrate, but soon found freedom in being able to talk with a willing listener.

He was eighty-one and had been on his own for eleven years. He had three children: two boys and a girl, the youngest son died a long time ago, and his wife eleven years ago. That was the last time he saw his children, at her funeral. Prior to that he hadn't seen them for twelve years; one lived in Australia the other in Canada. They didn't write or phone, so he was very much on his own.

After three days the young lady saw him peering longingly at a picture he had retrieved from his wallet. His head drooped and he dozed and was lost in his dreams. The young lady tip toed up to him and peered over his shoulder at the picture of a lovely looking girl, held between his forefinger and thumb, and she wondered what story that held for the old man. It was like looking back at herself.

The doctor visited and arranged for a nurse to check his cracked rib and his ability to move about. As day followed day the old man's afternoon doze became longer and he seemed to want to talk more. The young lady was attending a creative writing course, and thought she might, with his permission, write down his stories. They were never in chronological order and it took some time to follow the sequence of events. But never was there a mention of the young girl in the picture.

After coming home from attending her course one day, she found the old man distraught. She was about call the doctor when he stuttered out that he had lost something precious to him. She quickly scoured the floor without any luck. After some coaxing he confessed that he had lost a picture of his first love. The search continued and she eventually found the picture down the side of his chair. The old man pressed the picture close to his chest. The young lady seized upon the opportunity and asked him what secret it held. Over a cup of tea laced with a tot of whiskey he told his story of Marcia Ploughwright. They had met at a church event and almost immediately fell hopelessly in love. She was sixteen and he nineteen. She had come from a strict Brethren family and he from a Methodist Church and they would meet secretly under the ancient oak in the field. She told him that she was due to go on holiday with her parents and they planned to meet in two weeks when she returned. She never arrived. He made frequent visits to the ancient oak but with no result. He casually walked down her road, which was somewhat grander than his, and tried to look in through the bay window just to get a glimpse of his love.

Desperate to know where she was, he found himself following their next-door neighbour as she made her way to the shops. Hesitantly, he'd approached her and asked if she knew where Marcia was. She told him that Marcia was staying with her aunt in Yorkshire. Weeks turned into months and there was no sign of her. Time took its toll and his call up papers arrived, and war took him to foreign parts, to winning the military cross and being mentioned in despatches. Shrapnel injury forced him home for six-months. and when he returned to his regiment the war was almost over. On return he still looked for his love, but the family had moved. He threw himself into his career. At the end of his reminiscence tears filled his eyes as he clutched his only picture of his lost love. The young lady joined him, as she too, felt his loss.

Over the next few days, the young lady devoted herself to searching for the lost Marcia Ploughwright. The old man was not well enough to go home, and the young lady was reluctant to let him go; she had become fond of him. Her painful research bore fruit; learned what had happened to Marcia Ploughwright, the problem was how to tell her friend. Events took this out of her hands as the old man grew weak and the doctor's visit left her in no doubt that he did not have long to live, as his heart had taken a shock.

One afternoon as she saw him clutching his picture she sat by his side, held his hand and told him what she had discovered. His first love had indeed gone to her aunt's in Yorkshire. Marcia had been pregnant and gave birth to a baby girl named Helen Merry Ploughwright. Marcia had refused to name the father. The child was soon placed in care at the insistence of her family. She did not marry and remained in Yorkshire, dying at age twenty-one. The child had a number of foster parents and was never adopted. She was sent to Australia and after several years came back to England. The young woman paused, allowing the old man to absorb all of this. Marcia had never stopped loving him. And now the young lady began to choke back the tears. The old man asked what was wrong.

The young lady said, 'My dog is called Merry, named after my mother. Her maiden name was Ploughwright. She will be here this afternoon.'

The young lady showed him a picture of her mother in Australia, age twenty. They looked at each other and the old man saw in the picture the likeness of the young girl he once fell in love with. He reached into his pocket for his handkerchief and instead found in his hand the last leaf that had fallen from the ancient oak.

The Junior Angel stayed around long enough to see the old man's daughter arrive. The daughter he had never seen. They had two precious weeks together, father, daughter and granddaughter. In that time, he shared all about his daughter's mother, the mother she'd never known. Buckets of tears were shed, they laughed, reflected as to what could have been and, his daughter one side and granddaughter the other, both holding his hands, he slipped away with a smile and happy thoughts.

Tillie just couldn't leave and sat with the old man, his daughter and granddaughter as they held each other and marvelled at how life had come full circle. He was careful not to let his mentor know what he'd done to help bring this about. Sometimes he just could not help taking a hand.

*Fully Fledged*

Tillic was no more a Junior Angel. He had passed all the tests and was receiving his certificate of competence. Fully Fledged, he puffed out his chest, spread his wings and marvelled at the depth of the colours, were they really his? The great hall was lined either side, three-deep with angels who came to witness this event; he had scored highest on the Empathy test and they all wanted to see this new candidate. Were the rumours true? did he have blue, purple, the reddest red and deepest greens in his plumage? Tillic walked the long hall with his mentor and, his wings stretched out. And the colours, oh the colours, they dazzled. Other angels shielded their eyes.

He arrived before a divine light, closed his eyes and warmth embraced him.

'How say you?' boomed a voice and all the angels stretched out their wings, and in perfect time they waved them back and forth. The disturbed air lifted the new Fully-Fledged Angel, and he hovered there before slowly returning to the cloud.

Tillic felt as if he was in a dream. All the angels he admired most were there, even Gideon. With his Mentor one side and Gideon the other, Tillic was led to an enclosed space, a private place, a place where there was not even the hint of wind. This was not a place to be if you did not like silence. He would not have wanted to be anywhere else, he felt immersed in the silence. With all the 'Fully Fledged'. His coloured feathers were not envied by others as envy no longer existed amongst the angel community. It had been banished together with all those involved in the great rebellion. That, however, did not stop them coming to gaze upon his plumage. They listened to his stories of planet earth and marvelled.

He so wanted to be numbered as one of the Elite and had submitted his application for Warrior training and was waiting for a response. There was a flurry of excitement as reports came in of a distant battle. A number of the Elite arrived and were placed in isolation for recovery. They had lost a number of their feathers and damaged many others. They needed to regain their strength and allow their feathers to grow again.

He obtained permission to visit the injured Elite and listen to their encounter with some of the 'Fallen'. Each of them had lost so many of their feathers having launched them at the 'Fallen'. Having struck them they had watched a number of them wither and vanish, screaming as they disappeared. They in turn had been hit by strange black hot sticky balls thereby preventing them from launching more of their feathers. They now needed to be washed and cleaned in order to breathe again. They were dipped daily in an ever-flowing river from the throne room. Some of them had witnessed three of the strongest of the 'Fallen' escape. One of which was believed to be one of the strongest of all. If he was to be taken it would take many of the Elite, if not Gideon himself, to bring him down.

Their recovery would be slow, and some may never function again as one of the 'Elite'. Tillic left them in awe of their bravery and wished he had been there to fight alongside such Warriors. Perhaps he too would be sent on such a quest as they. As he left the Elite Angels to recover, he opened his palm to read that he had been accepted as being entered for Warrior Training.

There was a hive of activity as he returned to hear that 'Tracker Angels' had been sent out to discover where the 3 who had escaped had taken root. With their hypersensitive feathers and speed, it was hoped they would track their quarry and report back to Gideon. Tracker Angels were not Warriors they were seekers and searchers and would act in pairs to complement each other's sensitivities.

The Elite had been mustered under the direction of Gideon to roam the galaxies to pick up any reports from the Tracker Angels and deal with any threat.

Tillic soon learned that his Warrior Training would be delayed

The Mentor had received a report from the Registration Scribe responsible for screening all new candidates. He had read it and re-read it with fascination.

A new candidate had arrived before the Scribe. He had informed her that he needed to give her a name, and he scrolled down the list. This was the normal process; candidates arrived without memory or identification. The Scribe had to enrol them before they could receive their angel wings.

She rejected every name that he gave her.

'No, no, no,' she had said. 'I want to make people happy; it has to reflect that. I always used to make people happy.'

Finally, she settled for Hep'ee because it rhymed with happy. The Scribe was about to sign the register, when he stopped.

He looked up and said, 'What do you mean, you always used to make people happy? No one entering heaven comes with any memory of their past.' He looked her up and down. All entrants were given a new coat and their past was washed away. He checked her coat and the allocation number. He checked the size and the fit. It was definitely hers. He finished the registration, making notes in the side column. He had marked her report urgent and sent it directly to The Mentor.

The Mentor examined the reports on Hep'ee's performance from all Tutors and her performance in Angel Training School. He began to wonder how it was she had made her way into Angel training. It seemed to be her second home, her purpose, her destiny. What he found to be most fascinating where her report on visualising creation. When asked which they would choose to be the sun or the moon. All others chose the sun as it was bigger, more powerful, it warmed the earth causing things to grow and life to spring forth. It was the standard reply and earned sufficient points for them all. Then there was Hep'ee's reply. She chose the moon. Her reasons were that there was a great deal of darkness and the moon separates the light from dark. The moon would have a lot of stars as friends to communicate with and so would never be lonely. When people of earth looked at the night sky they would not be overwhelmed by the dark but would be captivated by the beauty of the night sky. Underneath its canopy lovers would pledge their love to each other and the moon and stars would look down and smile. It would guide ships to safe harbours and influence the seas. It would be nearer to the earth than the sun and easier to access, as the angels ought to be.

The Mentor pondered all of this and decided what to do. He sent for Tillic who was at a loose end. Tillic arrived full of anticipation as to his Mentor's plans for him to begin Warrior training and he was not expecting what it was the Mentor had planned for him.

'I have a commission for you,' said Tillic's one-time mentor. 'I want you to take charge of a new applicant. She has aspirations to make people happy. You may find it difficult and you will need a lot of patience, but I think she has potential. Her name is Hep'ee.'

Tillic, the new Fully-Fledged Angel, went somewhat reluctantly to meet the new applicant and viewed her from a distance while she played with others; all of them were laughing, playing silly games, rolling over. Totally undisciplined. Hep'ee saw him and came running to leap into his arms. Oh heck, he thought, this is not the sought of warrior training I had hoped for. He gave her a file to read and told her to be ready the next day, he was going to take her to some of his favourite places on Planet Earth.

They arrived to see Brian.

*The Helping Hand*

Tillic had met Mary going in the opposite direction, her face alive, clothed in white and with the broadest smile you could ever wish to see. They waved to each other as they passed. He soon found Brian.

Brian left the door ajar and walked out into the night, his cough had gotten worse, causing him to curse. He took the tall walking stick that his friend had made; it was a good one with a hook for his thumb and a painted stag.

Brian struggled into the night, with no streetlight to guide his way. As he walked, he began to sway; his friend, his stick, steadied his gait. He slowly made it to the end of the lane, his cough returned, and Brian struggled for it to abate, as he covered his face and looked longingly at the ancient church gate. He felt phlegm begin to rise, leaned against the wall and closed his eyes and spat. He drew into his lungs the cool night air and began to stare. He looked with fading hope towards the church, as he stumbled and lurched. Brian longed to make it to the gate, not wishing to be late; a promise made long ago to keep. An upstairs light came on and he hid beneath a tree, so that anyone looking out could not see. The tickle in his throat began to rise and he squeezed his eyes, pulling his coat tight around his chest. Brian stumbled on when the light was gone. He had made it, he leaned on the ancient gate, but no longer could his cough abate. His head hung low, his legs refused to go, he coughed and coughed, and his stick gave way and he thought he heard the devil say, 'You're nearly there, but you won't get there.'

Looking back from where he came, more lights appeared up to the lane and a door creaked open. He pushed the church gate, fell and struggled to rise and prayed to the God of the skies to give him strength.

A hand lifted him up and helped him stand; in the darkness he could not see who had interfered with his journey. The strong arm held him, helping him to walk towards his goal, and he began to feel whole.

His stick no longer needed to support his weakened frame, his cough had ceased, his chest no longer struggled for air and suddenly, very suddenly, he was there. Brian sat by the side of the one he loved, the friendly arm no longer supporting him. The moon and stars came out to applaud, and Brian thanked his Lord. His right arm and hand rested on his love's grave. Brian's breathing slowly ceased and he found that he was at peace.

Tillic looked on. Hep'ee held his hand. The hand that had aided Brian in his final quest to lie by his love. Tillic felt something travel through Hep'ee's hand into his, and he knew she would make it, she would follow her calling to make people who were sad, happy.

*Let the Training Begin*

Tillic began Hep'ee's training by taking her to all of his favourite places: the hottest and coldest, the most barren and most beautiful; to the rich and poor, it mattered not. There were always the sad, the desperate, those who loved and those full of hate.

Hep'ee and Tillic's presence had influence wherever they went, as Hep'ee couldn't stop herself spreading happiness wherever they went. She was always having to be restrained and cautioned about interfering in human conflicts, but her heart could not be restrained and Tillic had his work cut out. He started to have sympathy for his own Mentor.

They returned to South West England, his favourite place, and decided to tour the coastal towns of Cornwall. As they followed the Cornish coast it was Hep'ee who urged the progress only staying fleetingly at some places. Tillic wondered about Hep'ee, she was strange in so many ways. While he had no recollection of his past she seemed to drift in and out as if part of her had been left behind.

It was if she had another self. Words and phrases fell so naturally from her lips. Tillic wondered if she had fully changed into angelhood. Saying things like, 'I was made to make people happy,' confused him. 'I have to leave happy thoughts behind for them to have something to give them hope,' was her standard phrase.

When encountering earth people, she seemed to have a heightened sense of awareness. Hep'ee's behaviour showed all the signs of being on a mission. When Tillic wanted to soar and fly she would be tugging at his feathers. When he wanted her to sit and listen, to his experiences, she would fidget. She liked nothing more than to be helping people to dispel dark thoughts, let them feel the wind of happiness flow over them. He had watched her several times as some had chosen to end their lives. At Beachy Head she had stood in front of them gently blowing and then whispering in their ears. He had marvelled how some had fallen on their knees or cried or bowed their heads and to see perfect strangers rush up and hold them. Kind words and loving arms would lead them away.

Hep'ee was on the borderline of interfering too much, but he knew what that had felt like, so he gave her more freedom. This tour of the Cornish coast was different as he watched Hep'ee deep in meditation, a sense of mission seemed to drive her. As they approached a small fishing port, a sense of foreboding took hold. Hep'ee, whose feathers were growing faster than her wings could sustain them, was the first to feel it. She shuddered. It was silent and damp, the sort that brought a smell of decay. As they looked over the town, the sense of heaviness increased. It was as if the whole of the area were slowly dying.

They entered the town to listen to the sad tales from house to house. They sat on the residents' shoulders and probed their hidden fears. How the shops had closed, there were no more fish in the sea for the fishermen to catch, how the sheep and the young women of the town miscarried. Visitors and tourists had stopped coming to this once beautiful spot. Flowers died before flowering, and a sour smell drifted in from the sea near a rock the size of three houses. No birds nested there; it was barren. There was just a damp blackness the like of which Tillic had never encountered.

In angel training they had been taught about such polluted places. They were caused by those who were thrown from the throne room. Tillic tried to recall all that he had been taught. It was the one who became Light of Lights that had caused all the trouble. He was too popular, the most charismatic of all the angels. He took risks but always managed to come up smelling of roses.

Eventually he'd gathered a following that looked to him, rather than the throne room. The Light of Lights was elevated, and pride took hold of his heart, he started to believe that he should be in the Throne Room, that he should be the leader. Secret meetings were held, and more and more were seduced into his following. He believed he had the power to overthrow the Divine Light itself.

A junior angel had joined their ranks; he'd been known as The Discerner and he looked into the eyes of The Light of Light's and saw something that disturbed him. A root of bitterness had taken hold. The

Discerner lingered on the fringe and listened, holding within him their secrets. When he knew the time and date of the planned overthrow, the Discerner approached the Throne Room and begged an audience. The Divine Light listened, and the Discerner revealed that there were three within the Inner Circle who had fallen under the spell of The Light of Lights.

The Divine Light and those loyal prepared. On the night they were about to be overthrown, all was made ready. One-third of the angels, together with three of the Elite and Light of Lights, entered the throne room. They were met with a light so bright that they were blinded. When the light faded, they looked at their wings. They were drained of colour. There was just a dark blackness and a sour smell, and every rebel was taken captive and held. They were all judged and thrown out of the heavens to become the very opposite of what they had been intended. Light became darkness, joy turned into despair, love to hate, until each and every one was left to wander the galaxy seeking a home and a place to rest.

Tillic had later learned that his own Mentor had been the junior angel who had rescued the Throne Room. He had later been given the responsibility of reorganising angel training, ensuring that charisma was replaced with character, that empathy and deep, deep love of agapae had to score the highest for junior angels to become fully-fledged.

Tillic wondered if one of those Inner Circle had taken up residence here, and he wished that his Mentor was with them. Most of these distorted beings had been hunted down, but a few remained, and they were difficult to find. Wherever they had been exposed, there had been a sense of decay. Tillic knew this was too much for him to handle. So, he removed two feathers from his wing, sharpened the quills and sent a report to his Mentor. He turned to call Hep'ee; a report had come back to stay well clear of the rock, Gideon would be sent with a troop of The Elite to assess the area. Tillic went looking for Hep'ee.

She had listened to all of the despair, the heavy hearts, and was weighed down with their heartache, their sense of helplessness. Hep'ee decided to act. She thought she would gather all her happy thoughts together. Thoughts of her mother and bouncing up and down on the bed, the pillow fights and daily adventures. Her mom's uni friend coming to visit, picking her up and whizzing her around. Then all the happy thoughts of 'earth people' she had met. And she would gather them all together in one bundle. She would take them up to the hill at the back of the town, and when the wind was in the right direction, she would release them all and let them scatter over the homes and the people and the animals and flora and fauna. And like fresh rain it would fall and lift the cloud of depression and set the people free.

Tillic searched the town and considered what would cause Gideon and The Elite to be dispatched with such haste. He feared for Hep'ee, young and still in training and so impulsive. As he looked over the town, a gust of wind blew from the hill behind the town and a shower of happiness descended over the whole area; some of it drifted to the rock just off the bay.

Tillic turned and there was Hep'ee with her wings held wide driving the happy showers towards the dark matter. People started to emerge from their homes, children started playing, skipping, bouncing balls and playing tig. Their parents looked on anxiously, their eyes turned towards the rock and they started to gather the children in their arms and rush to the hill.

Anger emerged from the rock in the bay and grew and grew. It became blacker and blacker and took on the form of some ancient beast this earthly world had never seen. It turned and looked to the town, its people now scattering and running for the hill and the hope of safety.

Tillic turned to the rock and saw the Beast grow and grow, its hate preparing launch at the town and its people. He raced to stand between the people and the Beast. He knew he had to act. He spread his wings, bowed his head and faced the Beast. He launched all his feathers quill first, like darts. He sent in all of his coloured ones first. The deep reds, strong purples and powerful greens Each feather was anointed with empathy, love, patience, wisdom, joy, everything that made goodness and hated by the black monster about to engulf the village. They hit the Beast, some sizzled and fell, others pierced and wounded the Beast, throwing it back but not stopping it. It threw a great slime filled rock, hitting Tillic in the chest and throwing him back, hitting the closed church door, where he fell mortally wounded.

A child, unable to walk, had taken refuge in the Church and crawled towards the church bell and began to ring it. As it tolled the people on the hill, one by one, fell to their knees and began to pray. Hep'ee had been frozen to the spot in shock at what her happy thoughts had produced. The Beast rose to its full height, its arm like claws extended, its angry head raised, teeth bared, prepared to destroy them all.

At the height of its anger, Gideon and The Elite broke through having been spurred on by the prayers of the people. On Gideon's command they took up attack formation, heads down, wings spread wide and, travelling at high speed, he shouted 'Release'. Feathers shot from their wings. Thousands of them struck the Beast. Some burnt up, others stunted in their penetration, but many more got through and The Beast writhed and screamed. Its arms and head thrashed. Just then another wave of The Elite arrived and released all that they had. Again, The Beast fell back, wounded, hurt but not defeated. Gideon drew his sword and attacked. Emblazoned on each side of the sword in bold letters was, 'The Sword of the Spirit', and in one mighty swoop he severed the Beast's head and again in a great ark he swung the blade and severed both arms, then drove the sword into the heart of The Beast. With one last cry it screamed, withered, and was gone.

Tillic had been looking on with failing eyesight. Hep'ee awoke from the shock of what she had caused and flew to the side of her Mentor. She held his head, pleading with him to live, sorry pouring from her lips. Then as she saw his light begin to fade, she plucked some of the feathers from her wings and inserted them in his. Slowly his eyes opened, and he looked upon her tear-stained face. Then Gideon and The Elite arrived, doing what they could to sustain him. They gently lifted him up and carried him with them as they set off on their return journey. Ten of The Elite were ordered to stay, to ensure there was no remaining trace of The Beast. On their way back to the Throne Room, Gideon sent his report and Hep'ee, having been coaxed by him, sent hers, blaming herself for Tillic's life, which hung in the balance.

*Sacrifice*

Tillic was lain gently down in the Throne Room. Hep'ee stood by his side, wings covering her head in shame. The Throne Room was full as they all heard the story: Hep'ee's wilfulness, Tillic's sacrifice, the battle of Gideon and The Elite with one of the last remaining dark angels.

A voice from The Throne spoke softly, 'You may not recover; you have lost most of your feathers and all of your coloured ones.'

'He has some of mine,' said Hep'ee.

'But too few to sustain him.'

Gideon and some of The Elite offered theirs, those looking on offered some of theirs.

'Surely that will be enough until his grow again,' pleaded Hep'ee.

There followed a long silence that Hep'ee tried to break by speaking up, but Gideon put his wing in front of her and muffled the sound.

'Tillic,' said the voice, 'what you did meant that you can never be a *Warrior Angel.* You no longer have the strength. These feathers will sustain you for only two seasons. In that time, you will have to regrow all of your own, or fade'.

'He can have some of mine,' shouted Hep'ee.

'Quiet,' said the voice. 'I will come to you in good time'.

'But I can help him, I can stay with him and help restore him'.

'Quiet! A more wilful trainee angel I have never had.'

A long silence followed. 'Here is what we will do. Tillic, you will recover some of your strength here before being escorted back to Earth. There you will continue your recovery and we will see how you are in two seasons.'

'I'll go with him,' shouted Hep'ee. All the angels fluttered their wings.

'Shush,' reverberated all around the room. 'Shush Hep'ee, shush'.

'It's my fault' she said, 'if I hadn't tried to fix things it wouldn't have awakened the Beast and Tillic wouldn't have had to sacrifice himself; I have to help him, I have to stay with him and help him recover, I have to go back with him and help'.

No one had ever interrupted the voice from The Throne before, and silence pervaded the room. Heads were bowed and wings covered faces.

'Hep'ee said the soft but firm voice, 'stand before me.' Hep'ee shuffled forward and thrust out her chin awaiting her fate. 'What am I going to do with you? A purer heart I have rarely seen. But mixed with your wilful nature and desire to fix everything… it leaves you with much to learn. If, and only if, Tillic is willing to have you, you can stay with him for a season.'

'Two seasons?' pleaded Hep'ee.

'Alright. Two seasons and then we will see what we will see. To your credit, your action caused the people to awake, the church bell to toll and the people pray. You will return there and give me a daily report. Do you understand?'

'Yes', she said. 'Yes, yes, yes.'

With help, Tillic and Hep'ee returned to Earth, to the coastal town in Cornwall where, some eighteen earth-months earlier they had faced the Beast.

*Resurrection*

Flowers grew and blossom was on the trees; the sheep no longer miscarried, and neither did the women in the town. Children were being born. Shops were opening, tourists were in the streets. The church was open, children played, and adults swapped stories and laughed. The rock was no longer filled with foreboding. Birds nested; the sea was full of life. The fishermen came back with excessive catches.

The town committee had organised an annual trip to the rock. Tillic and Hep'ee followed them. The rock was covered with feathers, not normal bird feathers. There were thousands of them. And there, in a rocky area was carved an angel not unlike Tillic and by its side a smaller angel with a cheeky smile. It seemed the boy who tolled the bell had seen it all. Humans cannot see angels, but somehow the boy had. Perhaps some humans were closer to their maker than others.

Tillic sat on the hill and rested, while Hep'ee gathered stories from every home and shared the findings with her Mentor. As she did, his feathers began to grow even purer than before.

In the second season he began to fly again. It wasn't fancy but it was fun. Hep'ee and the birds helped Tillic fly, lifting up his weakened wing to help him soar or swoop. It wasn't pretty, but it felt oh so good. As time moved on Hep'ee negotiated an extra season with Tillic. How, no one knew. It seemed her tenacity had some sway in The Throne Room. Tillic slowly recovered, and he and Hep'ee experienced adventure after adventure that caused The Throne Room to take note and declare that a Royal visit was to take place on Earth.

*Some adventures of Hep'ee*

I thought it might be useful to you the reader to have some insight into the many encounters both Tillic and Hep'ee had during Tillic's convalescence and his gradual recovery to some 70% of what he had once been.

Hep'ee entertained herself daily by involving herself with these rather unique earth beings in a way that would not find approval from the 'Elite'. He spied her one day by a bridge sitting on the shoulder of a young man on his knees in front of a lovely lady and he held a ring in his hand as he looked into her eyes. A car slowed down, and a man opened the window and shouted, 'Say yes'. Hep'ee started to do cartwheels and Tillic noticed it was that man Robo, who he had felt drawn to.

She thought her constant interfering went unnoticed by Tillic, but he was wiser and more careful than she. Tillic recorded these events with the help of Priscilla the pigeon who would follow Hep'ee at a discreet distance.

'She's at it again,' said Priscilla. It's a good job Fully Fledged Angels can speak pigeon. They can also speak dog, fox, giraffe, cat and any number of animals, birds and fish. Insects, well that's a whole different story.

'She's at a funeral listening to Eric remember his dad as his ashes are interned. Keep an eye on her'. So, Priscilla went off looking for worms that were always around freshly dug ground.

Hep'ee experienced all manner of things as she spent time with Tillic passing to him some of her feathers to help boost and sustain him. Her travels took her to the sad, the hurt, those in pain, the devious and corrupt. She was exposed to love that would not let some of them go. She felt anger for those abused, prevented suicides and comforted the lonely.

Her feathers grew and colours began to appear. She wept over some causing feathers to be shed. The Special Boy affected her deeply, as did Puzzle. She had a hand in unmasking abuse. When a mother sought to outwit her daughter, she laughed.

She visited one artist after another to discover what it was that inspired them and found so often the creators touch. When she stood with an ex-soldier surveying the land from a high place, she to felt the love he felt for the land of his birth.

She sat with an old lady suffering from Alzheimer's, kept her company, awakened her memories for her to live in them and dream her dreams.

She laughed at the old lady making fun of the arrogant young man.

She held the hand of an old man wanting to sleep the sleep that never ends. Her feathers grew and colours deepened.

She shed feathers for the Love Child who became soulless.

She prompted a mother to write to her daughter, avoiding email and texting. She sent happy thoughts to her daughter to respond.

Oh, how she loved the two damaged friends, both hurt and in need of each other. Yes, she did a bit of manipulating in the process. It was duly noted. Tillic reprimanded her with a twinkle in his eye.

The young boy trying to know the grandfather who died on the Somme was led gently to know him. And how she wished she had been able to receive such a love letter that was penned to his love. She helped the struggling young lady full of jealousy to be set free. She saw what anger could do and how it could hurt and destroy. And how she warmed to the mature lady and her hopes of a partner and a child of her own. When she looked across this world, she saw the have's and have not's and those unwilling to share.

In the doorways of the homeless she sat and comforted them telling them of a better life to come. How she leapt for joy at the man's testimony of overcoming and for love to blossom. She played the song of Billy Withers as she saw those who leant on each other.

What she loved most was to sit with those who felt rosebudded and centred.

She came to share all of her experiences with Tillic, most of which he knew through Priscilla.

Read on, reader, of the life encounters, their stories, the best and worst of them. Look for yourself within these pages for it is you the reader they are intended for, so that you to can know what Tillic and Hep'ee came to know for themselves. See how precious you are. Hep'ee so wants you to see yourself.

*ASH (Eric remembering his dad)*

I sat watching my father's ash get longer and longer as it clung to his Park Drive cigarette and refused to fall. I wondered if there was a record for just how long ash could remain on a cigarette before falling.

His thumb, forefinger and middle finger had been stained dark brown as the cigarette smoke laid siege to his skin. He often nodded off these days with a cigarette in one hand and a book in the other. He had been clinging to life for years now. His heart, his chest, his cough had reduced him to relying on others. His wheezing chest concealed an occasional rattle and even as his body periodically shook, the ash refused to fall. A sudden bout of coughing; his eyes opened, his hand moved, and the ash let go of his cigarette, falling towards the ground. I reached out and caught it before it landed on the floor and threw it in the fire.

He continued to cough, and I prayed it would cease. He lifted his shaking hand, put the cigarette between his lips and drew the warm hot smoke into his lungs. How often he had done this and found his cough cease and his breathing ease. How strange that the very thing killing him also gave relief.

He took his last puff while I was away on holiday. On return I rushed to Selly Oak Hospital to find him lay in a bed with the sides up. He had suffered a stroke.

I said, 'Dad, dad,' and he opened his eyes, smiled and lifted his hand to ruffle my hair with those brown-stained fingers, then closed his eyes again. Tears fell from my eyes onto his weakened frame and my heart began to break.

He lay there for over a week, never opening his eyes, clinging to life like the cigarette ash. Then one night, when I wasn't at his side, he fell from this world. I wasn't there to catch him and tell him that I loved him.

The undertaker asked us if we wanted his ashes; we said no, we had seen all the ash we ever wanted to.

*A Special Boy*

I am a special boy, so my fathers say.
I am lucky, to date I have had four uncles.
They all say I'm special, allowed me
to warm their beds and stroke their heads.
School, they say, is for a fool, so I don't go.
Left in the street to learn and grow.
They name me nipper. Nipping here
and there, taking what I want, hide away in the day,
emerge at night always avoiding daylight.
I am a grubby lad gone bad.
Another father has arrived at my mother's home
And he has allowed me to sit on his knee,
to cuddle and kiss. Another night of bliss
awaits this twelve-year-old boy.
Wipe away tears and do not cry,
For I am, I am a special boy.
I have found a knife lost in a street fight,
It is my friend, held close to my chest
I caress cold metal. I don't want to be
a special boy. A grubby lad gone bad.
The knife whispers relief in its embrace.
I leave others to grieve for me, a special boy.

*Puzzle*

I heard scratching at the front door and went to investigate. It was an excuse for a dog. A matted, flee bitten mongrel, looking up hopefully. I turned, shouted the wife to come and witness this spectacle, then turned back; he was gone.

There came a shout from inside, 'What on earth have you let in?' It was a puzzle to me how, in but a moment, he had nipped through my legs to confront my wife with his head to one side, a whine and sad sorrowful eyes. I made to throw him out, but it was too late, those eyes had won the day.

My wife decided to feed him the chicken that was meant for me. This was followed by a warm bath and a rub down with a warm towel (something I never had). Whenever I approached him there was a low growl, but for my wife there was a waggy tail and he hung on her every word.

We reported this lost dog to the police and the RSPCA, but no one came to claim him. It was quite a puzzle how he came to arrive at our house. When we got home, we saw him fast asleep in a homemade mock-up of a bed and my newspaper shredded all over the floor. My favourite slippers were in his bed in tatters. When I tried to retrieve them there was a low growl, so I left well enough alone. As my wife picked up pieces of the newspaper there was a section of the crossword puzzle in the bed.

'That's what we'll call him, Puzzle,' she said.

When my daughter got home, they became inseparable. When she was seven, I passed her room to hear her pouring out all of her troubles while Puzzle sat there listening intently, a gentle paw on her shoulder. When they both came down for tea everything was fine.

When I was made redundant, I hardly knew what to do, how we would manage and with a heavy heart I took Puzzle for his usual walk. Puzzle insisted on taking a different route through an industrial park. He suddenly slipped his lead and ran in front of an entrance just as a Bentley was exiting the site. The driver braked hard and Puzzle rolled over onto his side. The car hadn't even touched him, but he lay there as if dead. The driver emerged from his car full of apologies and quite distressed. I picked Puzzle up and he looked at the man with those sad sorrowful eyes. It turned out I knew the man from years back. We were friends at school. He had just bought this new company and on hearing my skill set he offered me a job on the spot. I waved Mick goodbye and Puzzle promptly jumped from my arms, tail in the air and set off on his favourite walk.

One day my wife and daughter were confronted by a man trying to rob them. He hadn't counted on Puzzle who launched himself at the man biting his ankles till he ran off for dear life. The most amazing thing about Puzzle was the day my son and his wife visited. Puzzle was curled up in his bed when suddenly he lifted his head and started to sniff the air. He rose from his slumber and went to us each in turn until he arrived at my daughter-in-law. Puzzle jumped on her lap and began sniffing her right breast, growling. It became embarrassing for both her and us, but Puzzle would not be deterred. Eventually she said she would change her top and was gone for some time. She returned to say she had found a small lump. There was a phone call to her doctor followed by an emergency screening, and by the end of the week she was in hospital for emergency surgery.

I could go on and tell the story of how Puzzle saved the house from burning down, the hidden car keys and the chewed-up passport, all with a happy end. When my daughter was twelve, Puzzle could no longer charge up the stairs, so she carried him to sit and listen to her troubles. We were late back one night, and Puzzle was curled up with my daughter's favourite soft toy, my wife's favourite scarf and my slipper. He had slipped away with all the things he loved most close by. Puzzle came into our lives knowing we needed him more than he needed us. He had more intuition and discernment than any human I have ever known. Now that's a puzzle.

*Shout it from the Rooftops*

It was just like any other day in June. Warm, friendly and inviting. Waiting for you to open the door and step out into a new day with its sights and sounds, the smell of a fresh cut lawn in England's Vale of Evesham.

He was seventy and life had been good to him. Married at twenty-one, two children. After his wife's death he'd remarried. A lovely lady he had known for years. It was a perfect match for him. He had achieved his goals, fulfilled his parents' dreams for him. Brought up in a Christian family and in a respectful church. His father a senior leader and also a senior manager at a manufacturing company. He had been able to follow his fathers' footsteps and become General Manager. He even exceeded his father by becoming a Pastor of a church and he felt he had earned a good deal of respect despite early setbacks.

He sat in his garden with coffee and toast and pondered over the previous night's phone call from his sister. She had been in town, having a coffee with an old friend who had been in the church youth with her. His sister had described the conversation as stilted and awkward. Finally, her friend had said that she'd been visited by the police. They were investigating reported events of a sexual nature that took place within a church youth group many years ago. Dates and times had been asked for as well as contact details of any of those once in the youth and still in the area.

He sat, his coffee now lukewarm and his toast hard and dry.

He had been the youth leader then. Verses in the Bible started to spill out and overwhelm him, and always, 'that which is done in darkness will be shouted from the roof tops,' caused him to tremble. He shuddered;

despite it being a warm summer day he felt chilled through to his bones. After all he was only trying to help those girls, it was they who came to him, it was they who had the problems, wanted to talk, wanted him to pray for them.

He only wanted to comfort them, hold them, touch them, kiss-----. His mind drew a curtain over his thoughts, and he tried to shut them out, contain them, and bury events from long ago. What should he have done, turned them away? No, he had done the right thing. There had been rumours, but family came to his aid and they were dispelled. Although, he did recall seeing friends cross the road if they saw him. Others kept conversation very basic, quickly moving on.

He wondered about his first wife and if she ever suspected him of any indiscretions. The phone rang and he jumped. That was the second time that had happened, and he left it to ring. Suddenly the post fell through the letterbox to the floor with a thud. Dark deeds exposed! Who was it that had accused him? He made a list. He crossed out two as they were of the age of consent. That left four. Three had never married and he wondered why? One had been involved in several failed relationships and he thought about her. She had been his favourite. One had had a breakdown of some sort, but then she always was strange and that was bound to happen anyway.

His mind wandered as he fingered dry toast and sipped lukewarm coffee, which he spat out. There it was again, words in the Bible that came to stab him in his heart. 'I would rather you were hot or cold but lukewarm makes me want to spit you out of my mouth.'

It's been forty-years plus, why now, surly something buried so long can't come back and begin to grow? There was a knock at the door and he quickly shut himself away in the shed. It was dark and safe here. He always loved the dark. He covered his face with his hands, and he could hear himself saying, 'No! No! No!' That is what those girls had said so long go, but they really meant 'Yes.'

He started to beat his right knee with his fist and inwardly groaned. Why now, why now, why ever? It would be okay. It would all go away. The knock at the door grew loader and his head began to ache. Bang, bang, bang. He could see the judge's hammer fall heavily on the bench. The jury sat with accusing eyes, the gallery full of family and disbelieving friends, and those girls all sat together holding hands and staring at his soul.

*Unsuitably Suitable*

He's not for you that's plain to see.
He's not sociable, he's plain, not desirable;
his conversation uncomfortable. I wonder,
if he is able to keep you in the style in
which you are accustomed. No, no, no
he is just not suitable. He's too old and,
you, too young, he's too short, too fat, too plain,
you are tall, slim and elegant. He's too conservative;
he lacks get up and go, his gait too slow. Whereas you,
you thrive on excitement, new challenges. His eyes
are too close, his nose too long, he always has the wrong
answers. No, no, no, he is not for you.
You're 5ft 8ins, he's 5ft 4ins, as I have said before
he's too short and you're too tall. So, tell me
what is it you see in this man, what attracts you
to him? What's that, you've been on his yacht and
you've seen his bank balance? He has quite a lot?
His mansion, you tell me, is in millionaires' row.
He has a place in St Tropaz.
He is not gay
and his pacemaker is on the blink.
Well, I will have to think.
No! no! no! I have to say he is still not suitable for you,
but as for me, he would be a very good catch
and I do believe we would make a perfect match
and I would find him to be most suitable.

*Artist*

The artist comes in many forms. I am told it is in the eye of the beholder, this thing called art. Well, much of what I see does not impress me. An unmade bed I could see every day in my teenage son's room, a sawn up animal encased in formaldehyde, for me, cannot hide an excuse for art.
Who is it that claims to be the artist? The writer, sculptor, painter, the music maker, photographer, workers with needle and thread, those who do strange things with the hair on your head, glass blowers, planters and growers, the designer of clothes, painter of toes? It's open to one and all to claim the right to be an artist.
Most art is what we see; the visual has overtaken what is spoken, written. The visual has sort to replace words birthed within man that once awakened passion. Slowly pictures more graphic than our minds could explore have cauterised our senses and little by little by pre planned stealth has sort to steal the wealth of our imagination.
We are fed a cocaine cocktail in picture form that dries up the wealth of our imagination.
We all have a thought of our preferred artist, for me it is those with pen and ink, a blank page awaiting the creator's hand. For words to tumble out of one's mind, creating such pictures and images of life.
Storm clouds clashing from east and west,
Seeing a child lost on a park bench,
Forgotten and regained hope,

A restored life, a bereaved wife.
Memories of lost love, broken hearts, shattered dreams, revealed and restored.
As if some creator had taken a pen or brush and in a mad frenzy created in a rush – words painting pictures that make me laugh and cry or breath a great sigh.
Picasso's, Gainsborough's, Rembrandt's pictures in words to savour and satisfy my inner thirst.
These words calm troubled waters, create a storm, a volcano release and are able to bring inner peace.
Such words have awakened in me the things I thought were impossible to see.

*This England*

I love this land its cricket, leisurely played on country greens,
the willow and red cherry, cheery hearts made merry.
I love this land, its forest, the blue bell wood, its pools and reeds
and waterfowl who have made their home in its narrow passages.
I love this land, its landscapes, its rolling hills, the thrills of lakes
made full by streams that cascade down from heaven's realm.
I love this land, the tolling bells, its dells, the wheat filled fields,
the breeze causing strong herons to sway.
I love its changing seasons, the soft clouds in the sky, places to
sit and ponder this land's greenery, its colours, its nooks and crannies.
I love to smell the air see how loved one's care.
I love its people generous and kind, who are willing to give you
a helping hand lift you up and help you to stand.
I love this land that has given birth to creative souls, has allowed
them to breath conceive in their imagination words that can lift
you up to heaven and inspire a nation.
I love this land loaned to us. I love its markets, food halls and
farmers, the honour they pay to their beasts, the ploughed fields,
the way they nourish the land that helps us to stand.
I love this land, its coastal paths, this island that sprang up to
defy oceans and invading hoards.
I love this land, its strength to endure and secure for others to
stand on its hallowed ground.
I love its castles, its ancient paths, buildings that endure and
cause me to reflect that great men and women caused them to rise.
This land, this England never ceases to surprise, to open eyes
and I thank the Lord for this land this England.

*Who Are You?*

I keep forgetting – I can't remember –
give the wrong message to whoever.
People say 'hello' and 'how are you today'
I say, 'OK, but who are you'?
An occasional flash awakes inside and, for a moment,
I recognise a face – but not their name.
Their words ring a bell and I see the love in their eyes, then the
light fades and they are a mystery to me, the faces I see.
Time has no meaning, no one knows what I'm feeling,
I'm lost in a world of my own.
I keep trying to unlock doors, but I have no key
they are all shut tight to me.
I look for light where there is none.
The day becomes night, and the night becomes day
this fog in my head just won't go away.
I can dress and feed myself and go to the loo,
but I just don't recognise you. Who are you?
Flashbacks invade my mind:
I see a child on a park bench, legs swinging and a happy face.
A young girl off to the Tower Ballroom,
permed hair, war paint on, legs shaved, to meet her man.
Dancing, rocking, the smell of Old Spice, swinging to
music that only I can hear.
I feel warm sand on my feet, the sun rays and my body heat.
I see a woman who has laughed and cried
tears welling up and filling her eyes.

There's an open grave and a red rose in her hand.
But then there's this person who holds my hand saying,
'I love you mom.' Who I do not know.
Who are you, who are you?
It makes me sad to see her face.
Perhaps my locked doors will open one day and you I will see
and know and feel an awakening in my soul.
So please keep on holding my hand and hug and kiss.
I need that rope. It's the one thing that gives me hope.

*Wisdom*

'That's Elsie's chair, you can't sit there'.
He was visiting his aunt in an old people's home due to a sudden feeling of guilt. She had always given him wise counsel; he needed some now and here was this bossy old maid saying that he couldn't sit in Elsie's chair. Sod her he thought I don't give a fig, I don't care, she's not there.
'So where, pray, is Elsie?' he asked as he swaggered towards the lady, thinking it a bit of a joke.
'Better do what she says,' the old man that spoke looked like he was ready for bed. Old people he thought, they think they know it all.
'If this is Elsie's chair,' he mocked, 'where is she?' I don't see any name on it. He moved the chair to where his aunt sat.
She gave his hand a gentle pat. 'I think it wise to do what they say, or they will keep on and on for the rest of the day.'
'Look,' he said, 'when Elsie comes in, I will vacate the chair,' hoping that this would clear the air.
'That's no good,' the bossy lady said, 'she always has a lie down in the afternoon and she'll be in bed, in her room'.
Now he became really cross. 'Well, she isn't going to know that I have sat in her chair, is she?'
The air turned blue as the old lady tried to rise, reiterating her words as loud as she could. 'You can't sit there it's Elsie's chair.'
Sod Elsie he thought and sod you to you old has been, can't tell me what to do. So, he promptly sat in Elsie's chair and he didn't give a fig, he didn't care. There he sat and conversed with his aunt. Silence pervaded the room. Only the odd tut, tut, a mumble, a frown seemed to be around.

A strange feeling started to come over him from the top of his legs and through to his bum. With it came an unpleasant smell, what the hell? he thought. His aunt held her nose and others moved away; the old man's smirk would not go away. He stood feeling uncomfortable and sticky. 'See,' the bossy woman said, 'now you know why that's Elsie's chair but you, you know it all, you didn't give a fig and didn't care. You're like all of the young, thinking that because I'm old I'm incompetent. I told you it was Elsie's chair, and no one sits there because she's incontinent'.

*Sleep*

Sleep, let me sleep,
The sleep that never ends.
Do not shake me, attempt to wake me.
Let me dream, disappear, dispense with life's fear.
Do not raise an alarm, weep, scream and shout;
I will be where I long to be
Here, safe without fear.
Far removed from this life's woes
Carrion crows picking away each day
I once thought precious to me, which now I no
longer want to see.
Leave me on this hallowed ground
Let me sleep and dream the dreams of hope,
To sail across the crystal sea
To the far unknown.
Place coins on my eyes,
Kiss my lips,
Say your goodbye,
And let me sleep.

*Love Child*

She is the love child of a fallen woman and a wild man from the north who has no name. Conceived in a field of rapeseed oil whilst in full bloom.

Why is it shame hates the colour yellow?

She is the love child and her mother of shame impresses this upon her, squeezing her so tight that she cannot draw breath.

At night she counts the bruises on her arms and legs and her sunken chest.

A weekly ritual.

These are the marks of love on a love child conceived in a field of rapeseed oil whilst in full bloom.

'Who is my father, the wild man of the north with no name?' she asks her mother. A sudden blow and her lip begins to grow and then to glow. The taste of blood, warm and soft, trickles through her teeth, and that night she cannot sleep.

'This,' the woman of shame explained, 'will improve your looks, make you stand out in a crowd.'

'Why is it…' the love child begins, 'why is it I can put my fingers between my ribs?'

'That, my love child,' says the woman of shame, 'is so you can enter a life of fashion, be a model and wear clothes no others can and, perhaps, you will meet a wild man of the north too.'

Older now, the love child sits and ponders in a brand new flat.

Her frame, now strong, has taken on muscle and fat. The bruises are gone, her twisted lip has a certain charm. But inside her heart is still bruised, unhealed, her spirit distorted; her leanness of soul is there for all to see. She is a love child born by a shameless woman, conceived in wild passion with a wild man from the north. Conceived in a field of rapeseed oil, whilst in full bloom.

Why is it she too hates the colour yellow?

*Love Letters*

How to reply? I was told not to start with, 'I just want to say…' There is an art to letter writing, I'm told. Certainly St. Paul had it down to a fine art. As for me I feel more comfortable with Text or Email. But then, they tend, I feel, to have no, or very little, life in them. Dealing with facts, to the point. It's different with a handwritten letter, you have to stop and think and feel. Well here goes.

My Darling Daughter, I got your note, and I don't think I need to say, but, well, it can't hurt. Both your father and me love and cherish you and want the very best for you. We know you're going through a tough time right now and it's difficult to see the light at the end of the tunnel, but it is there, it is there. It's like when we have a cloudy sky, the sun, moon and stars are still there waiting to shine on us. You, my beloved child, are fearfully and wonderfully made, incredibly gifted with a warmth that invites and draws others in so that they feel accepted. You may not, my darling daughter, be in a position to fully read and appreciate this right now, but you will, you will. There is hope for a tree if it is cut down, that it will sprout again, and your tender branches will not cease. Even if you feel decaying and without hope, yet at the scent of fresh water you will bud and bring forth your boughs laden with fruit. I urge you as only a mother can, to bin the shame or guilt, burn up the dross of pointing fingers and place them on the cross where sin and guilt and shame are embraced and die. I would, if I could, reach out and hold you in my arms right now, but the distance is too great. Not too great for the love I have for

you. Hope deferred makes the heart grow sick but a desire fulfilled is a tree of life. And you will embrace life again, you will come through this, you will drink in life and spread your branches laden with fruit.
Bones heal easier than a bruised and broken heart, a damaged spirit.
Call me soon.

Your mom

*Friends*

Dear Sarah,

It breaks my heart to say it but I can no longer be your friend. Since I lost Jeremy it's too painful. Every time I see you with your four lovely children and devoted husband, I feel robbed and empty.

You know just how much I longed for a child of my own, but it just never happened and now, never will.

I intend to continue on the farm and complete Jesses' pet project of refurbishing the six cottages and Lodge and hope it will be enough to fill the void in my life. I will always remember our growing up as best friends, our adventures, your outlandish dress sense and how we thought you could be a model. But that's all gone, and we are both older now, you with your family and I with the farm.

Every blessing, love you loads.

Emily.

Oh Emily,

Oh, please don't unfriend me now, as I need you to befriend me more than ever. You see a loving family and Fred as the ideal husband. But the truth is I married a monster. Only Tom, now seventeen, was conceived in love. All the other children arrived due to Fred repeatedly raping me.

You have often asked why I no longer wear those clothes I loved so much, why the long sleeves and trousers and that I no longer go swimming. Well, the truth is, the long sleeves hide the cigarette burns, the trousers, the marks made from his belt and my back and legs, a combination of them both.

Tom has suspected the abuse for some time and last night he burst into our room as Fred was about to go through his ritual. There was a scuffle and Tom pushed his father over and threatened him, if he touched me again.

I tried to intervene and ended up with a broken arm.

Me and the children have gone to my sister's, but I don't know what else to do.

Sarah

Oh Sarah,

I'm so sorry, I had no idea. I'm bringing the big van over to your sister's. I know where she lives. You can come and stay here. The Lodge is finished and sleeps six and you'll be safe there. I'll be with you early on Wednesday. We can grab any essentials from your home while Fred's at work. Tom loved working on the farm the last two summers, so I know he'll be happy to be here. He could go to Agricultural College and I could employ him.

Please say you will come. I think we could help each other heal and have no need to hide our hurts and scares that life has brought us.

Emily.

Dear Emily,

Come quick.

Sarah.

*Remembered*

I never heard his voice, felt him ruffle my hair.
Never sat on his knee in his favourite chair,
Never heard stories of his life, his history,
Never smelt his tobacco or smoke in the air,
Never heard him quarrel with his children or wife.
But I felt I knew this man and how his life began
The struggle and strain to survive, how he worked
To keep body and soul alive. I visited him only once
Saw his name carved on a stone. He lay with others
So I knew he was not alone. Friends and comrades
in hallowed ground. Fallen together in a place called
The Somme. A telegram sent to his wife and mom
A sombre place. Full of silence. No laughter.
In this quiet place lay a soldier, my grandfather.

*I Love Thee*

I love thee, I love thee, oh how I love thee
I love your waking, your walking, your head
when turned towards me. I love to smell you,
devoid of alluring scents. I love thee when we
sit alone and refuse to answer the telephone.
I love to hold your hand and when we stand.
I love your boldness, your right to be heard and
how you smile. I know how much you have
cared. Oh I love thee my love, I love our walks,
our talks. I love thee when I see you scatter scraps
for hungry birds. I love your voice and the choice
you made when you said to me,
'My love, my love, I love only thee'.

*Jealousy*

I see the way you look at him and not at me. So what is it you see in him that you do not see in me? I've seen your gentle touch as you brush unwanted hair from his collar, your secret smile. It's clear to me that it's him you want to be with when you walk down the aisle. So why is it I feel like groaning? This growing feeling inside, I try so hard to hide and into a black hole I sink and slide and slide and slide. Counselling has revealed to me the things I failed to see, this seed planted in me that grew into a tree called jealousy. They say it came in through my eyes, the windows of my soul, corrupting what was whole, conceiving hidden desire, igniting a forbidden fire. If left undisturbed they say it will find friends to feed off and grow, laying claim to

what does not belong to me.

'I WANT TO CORRUPT AND DESTROY YOUR MAN, SEDUCE AND TAKE HIS WOMAN'.

Oh, is this what jealousy will do? Corrupt and destroy what creeps in through the eye. Search me oh God and know my thoughts today and see if there be any wicked way in me. Wash me, cleanse me from this parasite, help me fight, resist the allure, seek you for a cure. I don't want this thing called jealousy, this shame to lay claim to the person I don't want to be, to reshape me, mould me into Satan's whore. Is this what lay at Cain's door, what caused king David to fall in desiring Bathsheba when he should have been at war? If the eyes are the windows of the soul, help me not see and desire what does not belong to me, and set me free from this thing called jealousy.

*Anger Expunged*

Undo my tie and loosen my coat, something's sticking in my throat,
Things unsaid that I thought were put to bed, now words spoken have
raised the dead. Storm clouds gather like an angry crowd. Titan winds
meet from east and west, there to enter the contest. Their nostrils
blowing harder and harder. Wind-swept seas crash into the harbour.

What was once thought dead or at least well hidden,
Like an angry beast to the surface has risen.
Unexpressed rage once held in a cage, who dared to
unlock the door, was it prophet, priest or sage?

Words igniting a dead volcano, not knowing where it will flow.
A blow to the head, a knife, a gun, could not have achieved what
these words have done. A tongue unbridled causing such chaos,
Never stopping to consider and count the loss.

A bigger cage will, now, have to be made
And, in it, the anger and bitterness laid.

Or let it all out in a sealed room,
let the volcano erupt and the lava flow.
There's no counting on where it will go.
And if the unfettered tongue flows,
It may quench its song for a sweeter melody.

Pound a cushion, kick a chair, let that tongue stay still.
And stare. When all is spent and energy stayed, it's time
to let that volcano fade. Goodbye to the serpent, its venom
is spent, in its place for peace to come and words relent.

*Nature's Call*

Time running out there's a ticking clock, how long before regret is born?
A life within awaits, its clock keeps ticking, getting louder and louder.
Don't need a date, I want a mate to share my bed and stroke my head,
To see that the babies I want are fed. To always be there day after day,
not like some who run away. If I don't answer the cry of my hormone,
I could end up living alone. That damn clock, it's ticking faster and
faster, time running out, if it doesn't happen soon my life won't count.
Time to hunt my quarry down, don't care if his hair is black,
blond or brown. I must pursue till he goes to ground.

Where will I find this man, this mate, please God, not a Blind Date.
Time to look and sniff one out, put on my hunting clothes, the war paint,
shave my legs, wash my hair, my nails prepare, choose the right perfume
to attract my mate. Who will be the lucky lad, will he know I have need
of his seed, for my clock to feed?

Stealthily creep upon my prey, attack when he least expects it,
Make him feel like my candle he has lit. Time to weave my spell,
cast my net, see what man mate I will get. If at first a cast doesn't
draw him in, then again I'll cast it, this time wide,
And into my net that man mate will slide.

*No Excuses*

I must wash my hands, I can't get them clean,
I think it's because of all the things I've seen.

Babies dying in mother's arms
failing to register in the West's alarm.
Migrating people with nowhere to go,
Making their homes in ice and snow.

Must wash my hands, I can't get them clean,
Having seen the behaviour of the human being.

Death, destruction and fear from foe,
Leaving children with nowhere to go.

Taught to fight and taught to kill,
Given a gun to point and shoot,
Child-soldiers, arms raised in salute.
The torture of seeing blood-stained hands
Trickling down through desert sands.

Must wash my hands, scrub and wash,
I'm stained, unclean, the West's dignity lost.

We've plundered the best from the weak,
Destroyed their lives, the future's bleak.
Some have followed us, greedy for control,

Killed their own and dumped bodies in a hole.

My hands are dirty, stained and red,
With all the innocent that are dead.

'It wasn't me,' could be my plea, a poor defence
For closing one eye, while watching with the other,
The innocent die. Must scrub hard, I can't get clean,
God only knows where they, and I, have been.

Bleach won't work, to rid my hands of dirt.
To want all that others can give,
Leaving them with little and nowhere to live.

*Lost*

Sitting in a doorway with nowhere to
Watching the world dash to and fro.
No one to look and stop and stare,
So, they just carry on, sitting there.
Make themselves smaller and smaller
Holding the dog to try and get warmer.
What a waste, a disgrace some passers
by say, to sleep in our streets and create
Such clutter. That smell of a ne'er do well
They beg, they steal, make shoppers feel.
I'm glad that's not me. I'm an achiever,
Always on the go. How could these people
stoop so low. Each has a sad story to tell,
Of failure, giving up, escaping from the world,
Its concept of learning of working and growing old,
Hiding in the doorway, too much pain too much cold.
There's little chance of them reaching old age
The cold will bite, and sickness kill, some will
escape by taking a pill. No family or friends
apart from the dog. Oh, I wish there was a God.
They ran away from home and so much violence,
Abused in care for the grown-up's indulgence.
A damaged delinquent, no one understanding,
Left inside him bitterness raging. Left with no choice,
So escaped to the streets. Finding a dog, like him
Abandoned and raped. No hope now as the cold bites
Deeper, weaving its way through the cagoule. Feels
like drowning in an icy pool. Into the feet, into the hands,
Close the eyes to this sorry world for the last time
Will someone please, oh please, look after this dog of mine?

*Inhibitions*

Inhibitions I have none
Ask me if you will where they have gone?
I'll tell you first that I once had many.
They became my wall of defence, my shield.
They helped me to shut things out and lock things in
They robbed me of any thoughts of heaven.
For twenty-eight years I concealed my shame, my sense of guilt of sin.
I was 7 when these things came to lay claim for my soul.
Until then I had felt loved and whole.
Then Mr Childwell came into our park
Some of the lads thought they would have a lark.
The boys played jokes, teased and laughed.
He turned.
And I was too slow to escape.
That is when I learned of this thing called 'rape'.
I was left weeping, feeling unclean.
No one believed this seven-year-old boy.
Mr Childwell convinced them I was prone to lie.
That's when my inhibitions took hold, made me cold.
Then I fell in love with a girl and feared I would have to tell
About this living hell.
She introduced me to the man on the cross
And in time I was able to give to him all that I had lost.
I felt the shame, sense of guilt this sin be nailed in his hands.
And from the inhibitions that had shaped me I was now set free.
And I forgave the man who had raped me.

I no longer owned that shield of shame
Felt reborn, washed and cleansed no longer do I need to hide inside.
So come and see the man God intended me to be.
And what it is to be set free.
And I will tell you about the power of love
And what it is like to be kissed by Christs Dove.

*Lean on Me*

They danced
They talked
They laughed
She grew tired
Weak
Slow
The energetic dances became a slow waltz, no more rock & roll.
She had been to the doctors and then a specialist, then another.
The answer came back the same.
They met again, walked to her favourite spot at Towan beach.
A short walk along the coastal path took them to a bench overlooking the beach
They looked out at the vast expanse of the sea
They watched the sun sink slowly to the horizon.
'Marry me'
'No'
'Can I ask again later'
(pause) 'Yes"
The sun began to set.
'It's later'
'I know'
'Will you marry me?'
'Yes'
'Can I lean on you?' she said.
'Yes. Did you know there is a song called Lean on Me?'
She leant on him.
Two months later they wed.

She saw the specialist again and the flower of hope shed its final petals.
'You must never have a child' he said.
'I know'
They walked again to Towan beach
Walked to their favourite bench and sat watching the sun set.
'We should have a child' she said
'No'
'Can I ask again later'
(pause) 'Yes'
The sun began to set.
'It's later' she said.
'I know'
'Can we have a child'
(pause) 'Yes
So they had a child
It was twelve months later that Ellie arrived. The pregnancy had been difficult.
It drained her of energy then the birth. They did not believe she would survive.
But she did.
For seven years she fought to live, each year she grew weaker
Regular visits to their favourite spot renewed her.
She lay on the hospital bed, he on her right, Ellie on the left.
They dreamt of watching the sun set at Towan beach and sang 'Lean on Me'.
The sun finally set that night.
Father and daughter visited again their favourite spot.
They sat on their favourite bench watching the sun set.
Ellie said, 'Can I lean on you dad'?
They hummed the tune and sang the song together
Lean on Me by Billy Withers.
'Who do you lean on dad'?
'Me. I lean on my best friend The Rock'.
'Who is that? Have I met him.'
'I think it is time I introduced him to you'
'His name is Yeshua. Let me tell you how I met him.'

*Centered*

I walked the path from the lodge, receding fields to the left rolling down to the estuary inlet. I pass the final lodge and wood lined path beckons. The trees shade the sun as it snakes its way through the gaps in its branches. If this had been March/ April, either side of the path, partially hidden in the wood, there would be a carpet of daffodils and hidden fragrances would drift endlessly onto the path where walkers would pause and gaze.

No walkers today, late afternoon, early evening, just me, my solitude, my memories. Each step draws me nearer to my goal. I follow the bend to the right and see the main estuary below as it peaks through the trees, the sun dancing across its surface giving reflected glory refusing to be hidden by the dense wood. It invited, beckoned, called in promised whispers carried on the breeze.

Then suddenly, without warning the wood comes to an end revealing two bench seats on the left and the view, oh the view. Your forced to stop, look and listen.

The wide estuary, the sail boats anchored gracefully revealing the rear end of St. Mawes, a hidden secret place.

For twenty-five years I have been coming to this idyllic place. It stills me every time. My wife has a word for it, you feel 'Centred'. A lady I spoke to revealed to me that she felt 'Rosebudded'. What a lovely word. But 'Centred' will do it for me. I sit on a bench and drink in the view longing for time to stay still, the earth to stop spinning and to hold the moment of peace, solitude and silence.

The world can play its games of who is top dog, fight for control, spread its carpet of hate to engulf planet earth. And I just want to gather such power-hungry people to this spot, get them to look, close their eyes, meditate and dream of what could be.

I look at the inscriptions on plaques lovingly screwed to the benches:

'But pleasures are like poppies spread, you seize the flower the bloom is shed' Robbie Burns.

And 'Her memory dreams are here, her smile rests easy on the ripple of the wave and if you listen and if you know serenity you will hear her soul and the breath of the daffodils.' Abbe Searle.

I see an older lady struggling up the path from the quay. Every thirty steps or so, she stops, she looks down, drawing air into her tired lungs. She looks up to the gate and walks another thirty steps or so. As she nears the gate I rise from my dream like state and reach the gate before her. 'Oh', she says. 'Thank you'.

I invite her to sit and take in the view and the moment. For twenty years she has made this trip from Chichester to this blessed spot just to feel as I do, 'Centred'.

Hep'ee reflected on all her experiences, all her encounters, the highs and lows, those she helped and those she could only sit with and feel their warmth. She knew that she and Tillic would soon have to leave this remarkable place and its people. He was stronger, his dreams of being a warrior Angel would never be realised.

Hep'ee had cared for and entertained him with her mischievous nature and he marvelled at her close association with the people of planet earth. He sometimes wondered if she should stay here but he knew his old mentor had other plans for her.

As they prepared to leave with all their memories locked away within, Tillic spied Robo just getting into an old van, more like a Tin Can and he wondered what dreams he held. He turned to call Hep'ee only to see her staring intently at the man in the Tin Can. The man switched on his radio, and as he drove away a story of Archiving Space and all its wonders played. These humans, they both thought, and all of their imagination.

Note: Follow 'The Tin Can Teacher' blog and the 'Diary of a Space Archivist' podcast.

# *About the Author*

Eric lives in the West Midlands of the UK with his wife Jacqui and, as of 2022, they have been married for fifty-one-years. Eric has been a Christian for fifty-years, a Pastor for twenty-seven-years and a poet his entire life (though he didn’t always know it).

**About me**

I don't do poetry about flowing streams,
buttercups, wildflowers, butterflies and birds.
And what, for me, is worse:
To relate the changing seasons,
The flowing hills and dells,
A fallen leaf, a barren tree.
I just don't see what others see.
I tend to write about life, about you and me.
The things that make us tick
And the things that make us sick,
Humanity at its best and worst,
The blessed and cursed,
The great and humble,
Those who rise up and those who stumble.
I love to explore the living and the dying,
Those who suffer loss
and those who cling to the cross.

Printed in Great Britain
by Amazon

39204512R00071